Spirits of Place and Time

Poems and Stories

Peter Malin

In memory of my dear friend Robert Ball (1968-2020), who gave me the opportunity, briefly, to be a professional theatre director. His company, Fred Theatre, fell victim to the coronavirus lockdown – as, by extension, did he. Robert, you and your quiet kindness are much missed by all your friends.

Quaint
Device

Published by Quaint Device Books
99 Vanner Road
Witney
Oxfordshire
OX28 1LL

email: petermalin24@gmail.com

ISBN 978-0-9956593-1-5
© Peter Malin
First published 2021

Printed and bound by Print Design Focus Ltd, Witney, Oxfordshire

Preface

The poems and stories in this collection celebrate not just places but emotional landscapes and works of art. The spirits that haunt them range from people, both real and imagined, to the voices that speak to us from the living world and its shadowy hinterland. Eighteen of the poems were inspired by places in the care of the National Trust, that astonishing, indispensable British institution which has provided untold numbers of people with relaxation, enlightenment and solace for well over a century. Other poems, and one of the stories, evoke places looked after by English Heritage and the RSPB. If any of them prompt you to visit these places, or to seek out the paintings I have reimagined elsewhere, this book will have been a success. I hope you can find something, somewhere in these pages, that resonates with you.

Peter Malin

"Refuge" was first published in *Teaching Shakespeare*, Summer 2016.

"End of Days" was the winning entry in the 2017 English Heritage ghost story competition.

Many thanks to Lydia Hampson for help with my (non-existent) Italian!

The characters and incidents in the stories are entirely fictional.

Also by Peter Malin

Fragments: Poems 1968-2010
Love and Other Business: Poems and Stories
Out of the Dark: Short Stories

Revived with Care: John Fletcher's Plays on the British Stage, 1885-2020
(Routledge, 2021)

Peter Malin was born in 1950, brought up in Solihull and educated at Tudor Grange Grammar School and St Edmund Hall, Oxford. He spent his working life teaching English in Oxfordshire schools and completed his PhD at the Shakespeare Institute, Stratford-upon-Avon in 2007. As well as poetry and short stories, he has published reviews, articles and A Level study guides on early modern drama, and a book on John Fletcher's plays in performance. He has acted and directed extensively in amateur theatre and written a stage version of Dickens's *Hard Times* and, most recently, a dramatisation of the life, poems and stories of Edgar Allan Poe, *Why Will You Say that I Am Mad?* He has lived in Witney since 1977 but only discovered the beauty of its rural fringes during the pandemic lockdowns of 2020-21.

Front cover: The Eastern Isles from St Martin's, Isles of Scilly
Back cover: Lower Town Harbour, Fishguard, Pembrokeshire
Photographs by the author

CONTENTS

Dedications

Spirits of Place

Lockdown Landscapes

Daring Love

Confronting Art

Spirits of Time

Dedications

Unacknowledged

Liberation

To my father

He took it with him
In the quiet sigh of his passing,
A knowledge never to be shared:
Hidden, hoarded through life's dull drag
Since those broken, strange days
Of war's inconclusive closures.
What had he seen? What known?
Not much, perhaps, called as he was
To play his role when the show was almost done,
The unspeakable spoken, the undreamable
Dreamed into truth.
Had he killed? Perhaps, but by then
It was hardly necessary; death was surely done with
Here in these scented forests
Vaulted in unimaginable blue –
Despite the skeleton-rattling of the tracks
Shuddering beneath the trains' grim freight;
The accusing silence of impassive women
Waiting in line for cookhouse scraps,
Blurred in the volcano's blue-tinged breath.
What drama there was
Passed like a daydream, inconsequential:
Mussolini and his cronies
Strung up like meat in the buzzing warmth
Of the Milan service station, framed already
In the brown fade of the camera's memory;
The search for bodies, relentless, conscientious,
Each hasty burial in the pines' rough shade
Marked carefully for humane exhumation.
All this he confided
In tactful jottings of unpractised prose

2

Years later when memory's disintegration
Must have seemed – probable.
Yet, reading, there's a sense
Of something still withheld, some secret loss.
Even that one time he went back, alone,
He didn't speak of it, and no-one asked.
Now there are only guesses, vague as sighs.
Had war, albeit in its dying days,
Waked worlds in him,
Breached the horizon of dull expectation
Only to clamp him back to servitude –
The office, and the factory, and the home?
Names tumble from his memorising pen,
Tremble in the blurring heat
Of soft Mediterranean promise,
Strike jewelled glitter from the Alpine snows.
Naples, Pompeii, Ancona, Pisa,
Venice and Florence, Trieste and Padua,
Villach, Vienna: gateways ajar
To undreamed futures, unchosen paths,
Untold riches forever
Untold.

Entrapment

To my mother

Her "bad turns" she called them –
Those times when some twisting hand
Reached up from the dark
To clutch and squeeze.
Panic attacks, perhaps:
That slow, subliminal swell;
Anxiety's invisible abscess
Not quite at bursting point; not quite; not yet.

Absorbed in O Levels and adolescence

3

I was oblivious;
What did I need to know
Of loss or longing,
When she was always there
To craft comfort in home's womb-warmth;
Magic the drudge
Of safe, suburban shopping
Into the glories of the Sunday roast;
Listen, and love; validate
My faint achievements with reflected pride?
That, surely, was her job:
What could be missing
To cause the painted glass to crack,
Scored with the acid bite
Of sour recrimination?
I didn't deserve these pages torn
From life's seductive, lying picturebook.

Still, the bad turns got worse,
Rising from nothingness
To cloud the day's bright hope
With fear of something not quite known,
Not to be acknowledged.

Her doctor, a woman, unsympathetic,
Suggested she go home and make a bed.

Spirits of Place

Queen of Crime

Greenway, South Devon

The boughs sag, threatening murder
at every corkscrewed turn.
A darkening autumn sinks
into the path's thick mould,
an end and a beginning, while
the Dart's brisk glitter
shimmers bright dapple
through the leaves' fragile suspension.
The season laps gentle at
the dank boathouse, where bats
dream dark flight;
glows golden in the far canopies up
where the sun still shines, beyond;
shines on the foursquare rootedness
of the pillared house, fixed
in its terraced eminence, eminently English.
Wearied, foreboding, upwards
we trail trudging feet,
glad in the knowledge
that Poirot's deductive ratiocination or
Marple's unravelling of the tangled weave
will always return us here –
to the dozing hearth, the china figurines,
the armchair's enclosing ease,
the comfortable unwinding of the darkness.

Machine for Living

High Cross House, Devon

All I feel here is absence.
it's antiseptic, clinical –
but someone loved it once,
turned living inside out,
embraced the -ism, modern, functional,
clean lines, clear colours,
clean angles and white space,
permitting occasionally
the daring incursion of a lascivious curve.
Light plays in the rooms like a subdued child,
knowing its place, its required contribution
to the geometry of things.
There are no ghosts here: haunting is proscribed.
The dining room waits vacantly for nothing.

Outside, spirits call
from the circling horizon's dip and roll of green.
The house withholds an answer;
all its speech is spoken.

The Melancholy Walk

Saltram House, Devon

They gave it the right name,
this tunnel through remembrance
and green's damp fading.

Thoughts flip to a room, a dying,
and a drift of grief.

Screened from the world by indifferent trees
we're spared the city's lichenous, grey creep,
the river's single-minded, swift, slick glide.
We mute the traffic's roaring monotony of speed
to consider in silence the pet's unlikely grave,
the funerary urns,

                the room's forgotten scent,

the sad, slow dropping of the leaves.

Ahead, the orangery startles in white,
multiplies, myriad-eyed, the sky's tight gleam.
The air breathes promise;
a blackbird pecks its future from the lawn;
traffic hums;

              the room
is a room.

The D'Oyly Cartes

Coleton Fishacre, South Devon

You imagine them in sunshine,
the sky in its crisp blue shirt,
shadows sharp-edged
as the morning's razor.

Lunch on the terrace is a coolness
of lemonade and lazy jazz,
crabs cracked fresh from the bay
and a melting of warm bread.

Glutted grapes hang purple from the vine
and the hot border blooms blood
beneath the wall's distorting heat.

Face against face, the sea, the sky
consider resemblances,
squint-eyed in the shifting prisms of the air.

Distant, undreamed,
a road, a vehicle and a loved child
unconsciously articulate
their shattering convergence.

Hoard

Overbeck's, South Devon

Morning by morning
light climbs the slow hill,
waits at the door –
but its services are not required.
This is a house of shades that hoards
desiccated remnants, brittle and musty,
insects and birds and shot beasts
discharged from living, all glitter gone.

Turning to contemplate
the garden's steep descent,
light spreads its incandescent gaze
across the terraces;
ignites the reaching palms to green flame,
the clustering blooms to amethyst necklaces,
pendants of beaten gold;
scans further to the distant water's edge,
flaring to whiteness drifting sails
that crest the gleaming sapphire of the waves.

The Banana Garden's succulent incantation
of exotic Latin
conjures spirits from the startled air:
Musa sikkimensis, Tithonia rotundifolia, Hedychium densiflorum.
A brisk shower scatters the sky
to magic on each drooping leaf,
globing in crystal the reassembling blue.
The dragonfly, a mischievous, quick sprite,
strikes emeralds from the glancing of the light.

Drake at Home

Buckland Abbey, Devon

Time slides through time,
the world's far spaces crowd
to this room, this head; here, now,
the monks' bell rings for compline;
ships spit creaking fire raging
through Spain's presumptuous fleet
that flouts the Queen's peace;
flames from the future roar,
swallow four centuries
of quiet living in this Devon fastness,
presaging worlds' inexplicable conflagration,
Hiroshima's quick, annihilating flash.
Dysentery, scurvy, the endless ocean drag,
clashing of sabres and the stink of blood,
galleons, doubloons and tropic heat,
that final slide into the melting main,
swirl through the room's pale stillness:
unconscionable, incomprehensible,
unguessed of wife, of servants,
of the childless house.

Natural Magic

Tintagel, Cornwall

Warm sun, bright skies and a brisk wind bring me
Where butterflies bind me in Merlin's magic:
Red admirals, myriads, a mad kaleidoscope,
Feeding-frenzy of flickering wing-light
Jewelling in glitter the glistening nectar.
Unwary strollers, dumb-struck with dazzle,
Stand wonder-woven, tranced in their tracks,
Striding to Arthur's storm-torn stronghold.

The King has decamped, kinsmen and company,
His lonely fastness lost to gale-lash,
Merlin's wyrd-cave wetted with wave-drench.
Their lives were legend, a stirring of stories
To lift the heart-sick with heroes' high deeds:
A spell-cast of falsehood, fanciful, futile.
The brimming butterflies, brief in beauty,
Scatter their treasure – a truer enchantment.

Post-Prandial

Stowe Landscape Gardens, Buckinghamshire

Exiled, we occupy the pillared portico,
Shading our eyes against the westering sun.
We make our own conversation – women's talk –
Here in the Queen's temple, fingers and lips
Sticky with apricots, pineapple and wine.

Across the rolling, darkening meadow
The hazed silhouette of their masculine refuge,
Temple of Friendship, fades in the reddening dusk.
We hear their roistering, even to the clink
Of glass or goblet; the coarse laugh
Of some drunk politician; the effete whimpering
Of Lord So-and-So, whose wife sits silent here,
Smoothing the cream pleats of her satin gown.

Banished from Friendship – theirs, at any rate –
We find our own in thoughts, in talk they
Dare not imagine.

I study her full curves, her cheek's soft bloom;
Smile at her secret composure.
She reciprocates. Her eyes reveal.
I take another apricot; sip my wine.

Garden Slide

Upton House, Warwickshire

The lawn's end yields a shock:
an unguessed, yawning swoop of garden terraces,
striding headlong down to the brisk pool, then up
to the steep field's wide sweep,
rising and reaching for the fractured sky.

The green paths drop long and low
through bunched bursts of pink and yellow,
vibrant with flickering and insect buzz,
down to the dark shine of the copper beech
that casts its shade in mirrored waters.
Fraught ripples catch the sky's frowning,
scatter quick fish
to the lilies' cool sanctuary.

A geometric tumble of stone steps
spills and sinks through right-angled tangles
of platforms and balustrades, creviced with daisies,
a plunging stairway that twists us down
and down again,
under the spread cedars' guardian dark.

Vegetable rows cling to the slow slide
of their rich beds, black with fertility:
the colandered leaves of silver cabbages
waver in flights of fluttering white;
ranks of runner beans defy their name,
stilled on the steep soil, sloped on parade;
courgettes, inflated plump to marrows,
cower in shame among rough leaves
spiked with the optimistic yellows
of hopeful flowers.

Across the mirror-pool
a bulrush-jungle – reed-mace, rather –
its slow spread footed in wet,
shoots velvet candles, thick with threat,
challenging the unruly sky.
These tight, lush bowers, secret with life –
shimmerings of moorhen, dragonflies' quick flicks,
croak and splash of invisible frogs –
would never have yielded the infant Moses,
lost in tangles of verdant damp.

We look back, up and up
through patchwork kaleidoscopes of leaf and bloom and
autumn's thick-juiced bulge and swell
to where thin figures in tiny silhouette
stand where we stood, precarious along the top wall,
transfixed in the gasp of the garden's
unguessed, yawning, headlong swoop.

Sourcing Shakespeare

He that killed the deer

Charlecote Park, Warwickshire
(Henry IV Part 2, The Merry Wives of Windsor)

Inevitably they caught you in the act,
Raw-handed with the stricken deer.
Three silver luces (pike to you and me), staring askance
From towers and turrets, cupolas, wrought gates,
Preside like old Sir Thomas Lucy
Over the law's swift sentence.
Your flogging provokes revenge comedy:
Sir Thomas translated into Justice Shallow
For London's mirth, worth two plays' laughter.
Touched by celebrity, royal connections,
The only Shake-scene, toast of Bankside:
Were you forgiven the crowd's humiliating roar;
Invited back, an older, wiser Will,
To dine on silvered pike and venison,
Wry at the joke?

The spun yarn lives, independent of fact;
Its endgame: fame by association.
No truth to be read in the deer's inscrutable stare.
Startled, they caper pale-antlered, flashing pert scuts
Across the park's bleak greens.
The sun gusts cold in the gale that drives
Sweepings of blue across the skimming sky and
Troubles the Avon's rough rush.

Half-term hordes are fed the legend,
Flushed in the day's quickening chill,
As if they cared who Shakespeare was
Or why we need a tale that makes
Genius human.

Refuge

Baddesley Clinton, Warwickshire
(Measure for Measure, Macbeth)

Was it here that you conjured her, cloistered in singleness,
Mariana, restless in her moated grange?
Tall, red-brick chimneys, clenching clasped hands,
Channel her longings to an indifferent sky.
Enclosing waters, treacle-thick,
Lap the house in cradling isolation –
Consoling exile from a world elsewhere.

Or was it the priestly bolt-holes
Delved in the panelled comfort of the house
By Garnet, arch-equivocating Jesuit,
That spiked the barbed jests of Macbeth's drunken porter?
The knocking at the gate, peremptory words, trample of feet,
Rough, searching hands rating residual body-heat
In hastily vacated, fear-smoothed beds.

The garden-plot lies thick and clogged this sodden February –
But snowdrops scatter hope through lichened trees
Tensing arthritic fingers in the air's bite.
Birds trill their habitual optimism;
A chattering soundscape of unseen starlings
Rides the hushed rustle
Of vacant branches – bare, ruined choirs.
Ducks quack and clack and cleave brown waters,
Shift into ripples the sullen sky's dense cloud,
Silk-edged with silver dreaming.

The scooped cells are empty now
Where priests breathed slow, dark time.
The air awaits the sky's breaking;
Everything, tentative, stirs itself for growth –
Save Mariana's melancholy heart.

17

Home Guard

The Courts Garden, Wiltshire

Beyond your eyes it fusses, inadmissible:
your third war served
here in your bright garden
steeped in Wiltshire's sleek green;
Major Clarence Goff, pressed uniform
neat alongside the blooms' profusion.
Memory stirs the Karoo's fierce dust, flounders
in Flanders' thick, slack mud.

Smiling condescension from one remove,
your wife, Lady Cecilie,
collects waste paper for the war effort
from cramped homes cruel with the glare
of loss and grief.
Stiff at the cottage door she stands
tranced in memories of royal patronage:
the weak press of Queen Mary's gloved hand
there in your bright garden.
Later, obsessive, she embroiders magic
on the parlour furniture;
mind-weaves her Florentine *bargello*
into the promised, glossy spread
for *Country Life.*

Rheumatic, wearied, the platoon stand easy,
pressing thick prints on the tramped lawn.
Their eyes hold absence, duty,
quiet in these quiet walks
massed with flowers.

Scriptorium Vitae

Sissinghurst Castle, Kent

Who could say no to a room in a tower,
a womb scooped out of crumbling brick
and the light stretched taut
from window to window
to hang words on?

Silence,
but for the pen's imperceptible scrape,
the irregular click
of the typewriter's brisk invention.
Spread out below like an exotic quilt,
the garden's painted rooms
dissolve to green distance
where worlds' indifferent circles turn
and turn.

White Cliffs

Brides of the storm

The Seven Sisters, Sussex

Veiled in ivory shimmer
We await his coming;
Our green trains billow in soft folds
Far back to distances we scarcely dream.
No wedding-hymns herald our union,
Save for the seething waters' soothing lies.
Hands in hands locked
We front the land's fragile uncertainties,
A stilled chorus line, denied
The aching consummation of applause.

He will not fail to claim us,
Trident aloft, sparked with the sky's forking,
Tomorrow perhaps, or far beyond
The world's unscripted futures.
For now, it is enough
To watch the light weave silver
Through the sea's surge;
Listen to the waves' deceiving whispers
In star-strewn nights of ink and indigo.

Carved in companionship we stand,
Impatient for the whirl and stab
Of rain's crystal splinters,
The tearing rush and drive
Of the storm's taking.

Not the place's fault

Beachy Head, Sussex

My first thought is of
the land's transcendent beauty.
The cliff-face defines verticality,
sliced white through the downs' green folds
to the sea's thoughtless turbulence.
I creep to the edge, exhilaration tempered
by danger's transgressive thrill,
breath held for crack and crumble,
crashing the world's rim
down to the rocks' jagged indifference.

A tactful Bible text on a low plaque
urges restraint. Sad markers
line the air's yawning vacancy:
cross after wooden cross;
a mother's laminated poem
faded and warped in the sun's blind glare.

The jaunty lighthouse in its
banded livery of white and red
protects the seaborne, but turns its back
on despair's leap and plunge
from unsurvivable heights.
Impossible to imagine desperation
keen enough to power that urgent flight
to white oblivion, and the waves' caress
of crimsoned foam.

Ancestral voices

White Cliffs of Dover, Kent

The port's insistent roar
Incorporates the sea's bass thrum,
Conjuring war from Time's spent chamber.
Forces are massed on far borders.
Reverberation fusing into reverberation
Echoes Past into Future beneath
The cliffs' determined stand.
The eye traces a foreign coast
Smudged with threat on a distant horizon.
Giants of chalk, on guard, defensive,
Puzzle out paradoxes as the harbour
Welcomes with open arms wave after wave
Rolling in cloud from the ocean's other places.

A heavy drone, prowling, ominous,
Roars from oblivion; the Dornier 17
Stutters and plunges, shattering to shrapnel
The waters' heave and swell.
A skylark, startled, thrills upward,
A flurry of wing-whirr,
To heaven's high vast of perilous safety.

Eloi and Morlocks

Uppark House, West Sussex

"The Eloi had decayed to a mere beautiful futility [while] the Morlocks, subterranean for innumerable generations, had come at last to find the daylit surface intolerable ... Even the mere memory of Man as I knew him had been swept out of existence. Instead were these frail creatures who had forgotten their high ancestry, and the white Things of which I went in terror."

H.G. Wells, *The Time Machine*, 1895

"Troglodytic servants peeped [from] the subterranean kitchens of each house ... A housemaid came out of the bowels of the earth."

H.G. Wells, *Marriage*, 1912

A picnic on the lawn:
melodious trill of children's liquid laughter,
chink of teacups and the dull clack of croquet.
Lush, oriental blooms
blush vivid through verdant foliage.
The sky's sheer blue drifts warm with wisps
of angel wings.

Sipping your china tea, delicate,
cool in the stilled leaves' shade,
you hardly hear subliminal echoes
deep in the scooped passages
where servants trudge unseen.
Excluded from day's brightness
they carry back and forth the laden trays,
expertly negotiate the squinting dimness
of unacknowledged tunnels.

Only the housekeeper's son, privileged,
observes above, below, crafting prophetic dystopias
from inequalities: servants and served;
tunnels and mineshafts; industry's dark throb;
gardens and sunlight and the dread terror
of cannibal retribution.

Ellen Terry as Lady Macbeth

Smallhythe Place, Kent

and the painting by John Singer Sargent (1889)

As I raise aloft the crown,
a crepitation of iridescent wings
strikes sparks of emerald glitter,
caught in the lime-light's phosphorescent glare.
Plucked from jungles of the orient,
a thousand jewel-beetles
gift me their glimmering flight;
their wing-shards, flickering sprites,
spell magic potent as poetry.
Starlight, enchantment,
jade-light, envy's devilish sheen,
transform me into her, woman to witch,
weird as the sisters whose malicious tricks
have brought us to this point, this pitch:
ambition's void, the impotence of power.

Re-Creating Victor Hugo

Hauteville House, St Peter Port, Guernsey

Not a bad place for exile: hilltop-high
where cottages tumble
to the harbour's
bustle and toil.
This house, his reaffirming canvas,
rises story on storey
from Stygian dimness
to Light's patient waiting.

Each room relishes
its rich, dense *mise en scène*:
sapphire and ochre, thick pink and indigo;
tiles and tapestries, cushions and mirrors
and ebony figures.
Myriad voices, whispering, call to us,
summon us up through carved darkness,
up through the chamber of Death and Judgment
to Light's re-creating.

Alone in his lookout, his lighthouse-retreat,
he ranges the easy blues of sky and sea,
the jewelled, receding island panorama.
If on a clear day he squints tight
he can see France, or imagine
its stretched white ribbon
of lost ideals.
Casting no stones but words
he stands in his glasshouse, his eyrie of light,
knitting to closure the story-strands
of Valjean, Javert and the others.
Unguessed beyond the taut horizon's glare,
the future re-creates their pain
in music.

Damselflies

Chimney Meadow, Oxfordshire

Scuffing the fieldside grasses
in summer's high heat
I scatter pollen, dust
and butterflies' brisk wings.

Matchstick slivers of blue iridescence
tease subliminal awareness,
repatterned in each blink
to retinal flickerings
too quick for thought to catch.

Hooded Crows

Rosslare Strand, County Wexford

Buttoned tight in their light-grey waistcoats
They eschew the Gothic,
Exchange the trappings of crowdom
For the smart livery of a waiter at a wedding-breakfast.
A handsome pair, they leap and bound
From roof to fence to chimney;
Soar gently down to the lawn's green spread;
Glide languidly across the sky's azure smile
Between incongruous palm-trees.

You count them rarities, appreciate the privilege
They don't know they're granting;
Yet here, familiar as their dark cousins,
They're unremarked – even on boards
That celebrate wildlife worth noting.
They're hardly crows at all, you think –
Until their harsh croaks crack the pale façade.

Whitethroats

Fishguard, Pembrokeshire

Mist pushes into Lower Town Harbour
Where boats dumped ramshackle on dark mud
Smoke wispily under hot skies.
Time and the picturesque
Drift in and out of focus
To the lilting accompaniment of liquid song.

You watch them flit through cliffside shrubs
From perch to post in patterned strategies,
Aesthetically oblivious, unappreciative of scenery,
Marking boundaries with instinctive necessity
You misconstrue as music, melody.

The urgent trilling of apparent ecstasy
Tugs at your spirit, lifts your dull heart.
Clumsy binoculars find their focus,
Select their single subject,
Blurring all but its sleek perfection.
Beak stretched wide,
It flicks its throat to puffed snow and sings.
Its warning harmonies guard its world from threat.

Choughs

Porthclais, Pembrokeshire

Airborne ink-blots, too quick to question,
Ride the wind's roll to eye-blink oblivion;
Churring alarm-calls mark your incursion
Along the cliff-path clumped thick with thrift.
Just one remains, stubborn with purpose,
Catching your glance in its ebony gloss;
Its taut, red clasp of the cliff's fist;
Its bright spur of blood-orange bill
Jabbing, stabbing at spongy turf
To prise its grub-feast. Wary, alert,
It looses hold to gust and dive
In the gale's burst. Fractious, impatient,
Its young wait on your unseen passing,
Tunnelled deep in the hungry dark.

Avocets

RSPB Titchwell Marsh, Norfolk

You urged Norfolk on me
For my September break;
Whetted my appetite with promise
Of coastal jewels sparkling
Under panoramic skies;
Of noble houses set in stately parks;
Harbours and gardens and the backward pull
Of quaint old villages and seaside towns
Plying their business half removed from time.
All was in place, just as you said:
Rich-scented pinewoods stretched along the dunes;
Wide washes of saltmarsh, waving brisk with reeds;
Tight-walled gardens – colour-crammed tapestries
Burgeoning bright with fruit and leaf and bloom.
All these you gifted me, and more – much more:
Seals lolling hummocky and grey,
Unfussed and inscrutable on their spit of sand;
Spoonbills waking in a spread of angel-wings;
And avocets, your favourites, stirring from sleep
Knee-deep in the sky's dulled silver,
Dapper in the certainties of white and black
In an ambivalent world,
Up-curving bills raised ready
To sift the silt for survival.
For these I thank you –
And for everything.

Dandelions

Bed-pissers, lions' teeth,
on lawns they anger you; even in fields
their jaundiced shock-troops
stain spring's cool, fresh green.
Their hollowed tubes thrust up thick buds
from spreading dagger-leaves, serrated, dangerous.
Their delving roots thwart your trowel's keen blade,
snapping in white pus-bleed, a sickly trickle;
triumphing in their cut-and-come-again survival,
their instantly-activated regeneration; plotting
recolonization of the raw-patched earth.
However much you snip and cut
their vibrant Hydra-heads,
you can't keep up: wafting fluff-clocks
sneak through your guard
to take the breeze, take root and take next year,
leaving those ugly, naked, rough, grey knobs
to flaunt freedom.

But look again:
half close your eyes;
reimagine the blotched yellow
as bright daisies
shot with summer's blaze.
Eyes wide, we've lost appreciation
of their wild magic:
rugged crowns crammed with the sun's gold.

Promise

We are the spring: the voices in the leaves,
The yearning tremors of the troubled lake,
The chirp and chirrup in the busy eaves,
The throbbing ache that speaks in every look.

We are the harbingers of fragile hope:
The tender greening of the wayside verge
Promising blossom is within our scope,
And bluebells, gathered for the ready vase.

We brush the sky with hints of richer blue,
And thaw the pain in fingers stiff with cold;
We word reminders of the things you knew
But counted lost, until the voices called.

spring break

... I arrive at a new place / a window
stands open / seas pound
under turbulent stars / unknown ghosts
jostle for introductions / morning
slips through unhurried curtains /
new buds peel into green and
finger the sky's vacancy / a girl
in pink-framed glasses delivers
my frothed coffee / enjoy ...

Life on Facebook

This is my cat
I love my cat
She purrs and hisses
And stuff like that
My cat

This is my goldfish
Floating goldfish
Dead in its bowl
It was quite an old fish
Cold fish

This is my lunch
Tasty lunch
Sticks of raw carrot
Give a lovely crunch
To lunch

This is my knife
Nice sharp knife
Slices through carrot
Then slices through life
My knife

This is my blood
Bright red blood
Pools on the lino
A thickening flood
Hot blood

This was my life
Facebook life
Cat carrot goldfish
Blood from the knife
Great life

In the Supermarket

a different world

rambutan, okra,
romanesco cauliflower
pak choi, passion fruit,

kiwi, papaya:
weird, exotic fantasies
undreamed in childhood

food fight

it's a war out there.

custard *slices*, cocoa *pops*,
tortilla *chips*, fruit *drops*,
pasta *shells*, lamb *chops*;

sugar *puffs*, milk *shakes*,
sausage *rolls*, corn *flakes*,
rhubarb *crumbles*, coffee *breaks*.

RUN FOR YOUR LIVES!

Blue Plaque

on this site
sometime in the past
some people lived
whose views are unacceptable today
because they lived
sometime in the past
and have therefore been erased
from history

paradox

in my room I escape
the worldwide pandemic

wither

and die

Winter Breathing

The Rack Isle, Bibury, Gloucestershire

Somewhere amidst the stacked coaches, ice-cream vans,
tramp and shuffle of summer's jostling ghosts,
the Coln's cool ripple, squeezed to thin glitter,
frames in its flow this fragile, postage-stamp wildness –
ordinary, uninspiring, unremarked.

Now in January I park easy,
breathe, fresh and free, the clouds' damp swirl.
Rustlings of rough-tangled grasses
tease with hints of hidden life:
subliminal flick-flit of brisk-winged birds;
the trout's sleek glide
half-glimpsed in the sky's self-regard;
the water-vole's passing, printed in transience.
Years past, drained drought-dry,
all was crack and dust-crumble;
now, reeds and weeds, mosses and sucking mud
absorb the day's grey chill,
celebrate the season's gaunt branches
flickering with birdsong.

Postcards from Buxton, May 2019

The Crescent

The builders are in –
But hoardings and hard hats, diggers and dust,
Fail to defile the clean, curved sweep
Of Georgian elegance.
Ghosts of the well-to-do
Gather in gutted rooms,
Pace the long corridors of strewn rubble.

They came to take the waters,
Healing, preservative;
But miracles cannot outlast old age,
And restoration is
A temporary state.

The Devonshire Dome

Pressed to insignificance
By height and space,
We lift our gaze
Upwards and upwards
Into the domed vault's
Irrational expansion.

Dead centre, a hand-clap cracks thunder
Across the vast canopy of light,
Pressing the universe
Upwards and upwards.

The Church of St Anne

Surely not worth a glance,
This squat grey shed of a church
Tucked snug in its side-street.
Yet its dark door
Opens on wonders of art and artistry:
Exquisite, modest, worth a moment's pause.

Pause, too, in the hummocky, cramped churchyard
Of splintering graves – all looking east
But one: John Kane, comedian,
Dead funny,
Facing his audience –
Still.

Pavilion Gardens

Eden falls away from the Broad Walk's
Tree-lined elegance, a lush arboretum
Of lawns and lakes, rife with rhododendrons
Blushing their secrets in purple and crimson.
The damp Bank Holiday draws crowds
Of Canada Geese, printing their webbed rule
In softened turf, asserting ownership
In oil-paint swirls of green and grey.
We tread here at our peril, marching
To the bandstand's strained jollity,
While Punch and Judy's grim, abusive marriage
Draws innocent laughter through the knowing air.

The Octagon

Ghosts everywhere...

Amidst the craft-fair crowds, buzzing
For Bank Holiday bargains,
The early Beatles take the stage,
Far from the dense, smoky fug
Of their Liverpool Cavern:
Aliens in this geometric Victorian pavilion
Of domed glass.

Stilled phantoms in 1960s black-and-white,
They pound their raucous, silent music
To screaming, silent crowds –
'Please please me' the evening's urgent, polite demand.
Caught forever in the moment's heavy beat,
They hang framed for the future's
Moderately-interested gaze.

The Opera House

These days it's all about the play:
The auditorium a mere black box,
Blank canvas for the conjuring of dreams.
For Matcham, though, the medium was the message:
The building itself the Art that shifts
Imagination to a different sphere.

Here, in a town of domes,
They crown the theatre too: Byzantium made English.
Entering the House, sacred to magic, we marvel first
At the ceiling's baroque extravagance.
Never mind the show, (tonight it's *Oliver!*);
Cast up your eyes instead to sculptured fantasies,
Rendered exquisitely in cream and gold.

Solomon's Temple, Poole's Cavern

Custodian of the viewpoint,
You command the peaks:
Picturesque folly perched atop
These greened and landscaped heaps
Of waste and slag.

Beneath, the sculpted chambers
Drip limestone fantasies;
The guide, a stand-up *manqué*,
Spins tales of wonder for chilled tourists.

Below, huddled in the hills' soft dip,
The town sleeps in mist:
Dome and Pavilion, Opera House and Crescent,
Mere faintness in a dim and distant dream.

Isles of Scilly

Hell Bay, Bryher

Shifting diamonds of blue steel
surge and retreat in the sea's heave and swell,
flick foam-crests brief as beauty
up into bright air.
The keen Atlantic flings its dark heft
in hurl and spray-crash,
skirting in white the black stacks
of jumbled boxes guarding the stern cliffs,
battered, beleaguered, rugged with rockfall.
Sweeps and folds of waved heath
rise to the sky's summons,
clumped soft and pink with thrift.

Limited edition

This place intensifies the facts of living.
Contexts switch in a glance, a blink.
A quick turn, the breath of a breeze,
a bird's swift dash from orange to scarlet
confer uniqueness on the moment:
each view, each vista,
differently angled, newly perspectived,
gifted to us alone.
Skies shift; the sea's split blues
brush at the blind whites of the hot beach;
new buds break brilliant,
colliding colours across the sharp air.
The scene's components mesh and fix,
each instant printed once, once only.

The whole world works like this –
but here, we notice.

Valhalla figureheads, Tresco Abbey Gardens

Upper bodies thrust voluptuously
Out across an absent ocean,
These carved white goddesses, blank-eyed, remote,
Exude complacency,
Minds wiped of loss, and wreck.

More humble, human figures draw the eye,
Etched with inner life:
The homely matron, plump-cheeked, ordinary,
Harbouring the quiet ecstasy of a mother's love;
This Puritan lady, provocatively auburn,
Pinched in pale blue, with her pink rose;
That dark-haired girl, dreaming passion,
Clasping to her breast the bloom's crimson;
The dashing officer, barely a man,
His raised blade poised to uncrest the waves.
Their eyes tell all,
Thought-torn between past and future:
Ahead, the intolerable excitement of the voyage,
Cleaving the pounding seas to dashed spray;
Behind, those loved and left –
The family praying for a safe return;
The children, troubled in their cradled sleep;
The lover, weeping for the shrivelled rose.

> the wind's message whirls and slaps our faces,
> its salt rush torn from atlantic turmoil's flashing steel,
> ripped from the sea's chapped lips in a spouting of
> spray

> white rain flies horizontal across scoured rocks
> like tumbled seaweed dashed down the swept beach

> we cling to hope,
> despite the gale's sharp threat and the salt's sting;
> despite the shrill inevitability of our splintering end

Lockdown Landscapes

Walks from my house, 2020

Witney, Oxfordshire

"After-comers cannot guess the beauty been.
Ten or twelve, only ten or twelve
Strokes of havoc únselve
The sweet especial scene,
Rural scene, a rural scene,
Sweet especial rural scene."

Gerard Manley Hopkins, "Binsey Poplars"

Opening Window

Beyond my garden, winter's clogged soil
shoots fresh with promise of a new crop.
The fields rise to hedgerows and copses
sun-sharp in spring's infinities of green.

Red kites swirl and soar,
etched russet and chestnut
on the sky's miraculous blue,
oblivious of their kingdom's planned destruction.

I, though – glorying in
the rise and roll of rich earth,
the trill of skylarks and the cuckoo's call –
superimpose my knowing on the scene,
praying never to see the day
the diggers crash in, wreaking their revenge
on Nature's priceless, blameless paradise.

Nimby

All moralities
are awkward, ambivalent,
shaded in nuance.

Forty years ago,
while the land slept, undreaming
of desecration,

someone else stood here,
breathing the world's calm beauty,
where my home now stands.

Should I then accept
the charge of hypocrisy:
"Not in *my* back yard"?

The answer lies there,
in the earth's exploding green
and the skylark's song.

Foxburrow Wood

The kestrel's poise locks the landscape
in precise scrutiny. Focused on prey,
its sharpened, hovering gaze indifferently eyes
the greening land's soft slope;
the careful compositions of maturing trees
aesthetically arranged to capture naturalness;
the hollowed pool, still rough with tumbled rocks;
the stream's trickling thread,
its daffodil fringe dotted with gold.

This ersatz treescape, "community wood",
is none the worse for its romanticised vision
of what we need from Nature:
the stream criss-crossed
by rustic bridges, artful stepping-stones;
paths planned to maximise the view,
leading us gently to the gate
that grants our souls both access and egress.

Some time ahead, when life unlocks
and the kestrel's scan detects danger,
the spread of urban sprawl will reach here, almost,
stretching its concrete grasp to Eden's rim.

Waking World

The land ghosts itself in its slow breathing,
hazed in the sun's luminous gaze.
The ancient meadows, wheat- and barley-rich,
their destined livery of massed housing
delayed by lockdown,
wake to the morning, sing every shimmer
of spring's soft airs.
Skylarks ascend on whirring wings,
thrilling the air with cascading song,
invisible in the sky's immensities
of deepening blue.

In the field at the top of Foxburrow Wood
a massed scampering of early rabbits
stops me short in its unexpectedness.
I count thirty at least before,
sensing my watching presence,
they freeze and melt into the brown grass.

Windrush Water-Meadows

As month follows month
the meadows reinvent themselves,
wrung dry in the sun's unsparing grip.
Pools parch to mud, mud to cracked ruts,
stumbling clumsy feet beside
the river's slow, meandering, reedy banks.

April's lazy breezes set the bright lanes dancing
in drifts of white lace.
May's massed ranks raise cups of glowing gold
aloft in celebration.
In June, swathed heads of whisked cream
froth their sweet scent through the stilled air.
July parades the imperial guard
in clustered spikes of regal purple.

Ducklings are hatched in fluff;
in a quick day, swallows are magicked back
to skim and sweep the river's darts and swirls;
dragonflies flick and whirr their brilliance
in blinks of cobalt, jet and emerald.

Secret birds, cooled in leaf-shade,
compete to have their voices recognised
by ignorant ears,
while crickets chirrup shimmering
through infinite variations on the theme of grass.

A lone heron lopes lazily along the sky,
skirts the willows' drooping sadness,
settles, scans, switches to sleep-mode,
grey statue in the wide and waving green.

Rising from the meadows' verdant, beating heart
the half-built housing estate hangs in threat
on the steep hillside.
From across the valley its scar blights the scene,
whose perfectness is now forever
únselved
in reckless vandalism.
Rumour whispers that work was halted
when houses subsided down the trembling slope.
Secretly I smile, and turn my back to view
what still remains of beauty.

Cormorant

on Witney Lake,
the roar of the bypass silenced, Covid-stilled,
a black angel spreads its wings
wide to the drying sun,
scatters flung droplets in glittering arcs

as Time slows, opens a shutter
to past days, another place,
a moment missed, a door closed,
a white beach, a rugged coast,
where a black angel spreads its wings
wide to the drying sun,
scatters flung droplets in glistening arcs

that bring me here
to now, to nowhere,
the quiet lake, the dark trees,
the blank sky, the walk home,
the roar of the bypass silenced, Covid-stilled.

Indecencies

The concrete platform fronts the waterside,
broken, weed-cracked,
a boatless wharf on an unnavigable river.
An information board, faded and stained,
reveals its history: the old bathing-house,
Victorian Witney's tactful attempt
to curb indecency.
Long-demolished, the changing cubicles
promoted privacy, offered discouragement
to "persons exposing themselves in a state of nudity"
along the river's prudish banks.

Rising behind the protective grotto of gloomy trees,
bright new houses spread brick and tarmac
across the hillside to the locked-down,
half-built, excavated scar
that gazes complacently
across the water-meadows.

Odd that we preserve the concrete slab,
but not the landscape.

Skeletons

Minster Lovell Hall

"A skeleton form lay mouldering there
In the bridal wreath of that lady fair."
                                    Thomas Haynes Bayley, "The Mistletoe Bough"

Clustered ruins, huddled in mysteries,
crack grey in the day's hot blue –
skeleton-haunted, cloistered in quietness.

Rippling dark through dim woods
the Windrush speaks secrets,
legend and history fused into cryptogram
in its archaic tongue.
Meanings are locked in the crumbling stones
like the mummified bride in the old oak chest
or the skeleton starved in the basement room.

Discrediting fictions is easy enough,
but truth lies irrecoverable,
breeding hydra-headed speculation,
bristling with tongues
like Rumour in the old moralities
of medieval drama.

The place is quiet enough
now, in the humid day.
At night who knows what whispers pass between
the river's eddy and the rustling trees,
the flitting bats and prescient, ghosting owls?

Interventions

All moralities
are awkward, ambivalent,
shaded in nuance.

These landscapes exist
through human intervention:
the streams and copses,

lanes and bridleways;
the meadows' trembling grasses
and the fertile earth.

Are they fair game, then –
mere collateral damage,
profit's casualties?

The answer lies there,
in the river's gentle rush
and the swallow's grace.

Vision

What does the owl dream in its prescience?
From ruin's high perch
its wisdom scans the future,
peering clear-eyed far down the crushed valley
cramped in its parallel bars of brick
almost as far as the town itself:
the blanket-mill's surviving, smokeless chimney
and the faint spire of St Mary's Church,
hands pressed together in despairing prayer.

The river still runs,
flooding its flat reaches with the stink of sewage,
past the concrete plinth of the old bathing-house
which still exists because, frankly,
what else would you put there?

Beyond the church, completing the view,
three matching towers of concrete homes
triangulate the jaded lake
where the roar of the un-stilled bypass silences
skylark and cricket and all the voices
of the waving meadows.
Atop each tower, a black angel spreads its wings
wide to the drying sun,
scattering flung droplets in glistening arcs
of tears.

Autumn Shutdown

blustering gales whip sharp tears
from the trees' heaviness

torn skies weep to mud
the curdled paths

life hangs hidden in sodden boughs,
struck sad and silent in the season's
shrill, inexorable screaming of wind and rain

a shaft of gold
splits the clouds' canopy
in angry recrimination:
a dazzle of hope,
ineffective and momentary,
as the air breathes closure
through darkening leaves

Daring Love

"Never durst poet touch a pen to write
Until his ink were tempered with Love's sighs."

William Shakespeare, *Love's Labour's Lost*

"And indeed there will be time
To wonder, 'Do I dare?' and, 'Do I dare?'
Time to turn back and descend the stair,
With a bald spot in the middle of my hair –"

T. S. Eliot, "The Love Song of J. Alfred Prufrock"

"I am the love that dare not speak its name."

Lord Alfred Douglas, "Two Loves"

unattainable

I admire you from afar
across oblivious crowds
of chattering students.
Sleek and handsome in
your casual get-up of tight
black jeans and white
T-shirt
you catch my eye
and smile.

You shift me back in time
to the boy at school I fancied
(though that's not a word
I could have chosen then)
who I followed home each day
but never spoke to,
sore with inexplicable longing.

More confident now, more knowing,
I make a beeline for
your advertised accessibility, and start
what turns out to be
a far from awkward conversation.
You're friendly, natural, open;
does it matter if
your interest in me goes no further?
It's a start at least,
an opening door, a half-glimpsed path,
a road that may lead somewhere
if I take it

discovery

we passed in secret through
the door we dared to open
and took the quiet path
fringed with spring flowers and
the rich hues of autumn –
an easy path after we'd
successfully negotiated
the awkward nettle-patch
of our first kiss
that led us – not quite prepared –
to the discovery of passion
on that golden evening
of sunset after rain
and the slow unpeeling
of inhibition
that left us knowing
there was nothing between us
that couldn't be dreamed
or said

together

As we skirt the field's edge, scuffing dust,
you take my hand,
a calculated risk,
conferring wholeness for the briefest spell.

Above us, disregarding
our temporary oneness,
a pair of red kites dance
their leisurely, slow swirl.
They have their purposes, we ours,
in the world's separating currents.

Later, alone, I struggle with a poem.
Words break into wrong shapes,
fail to join as our hands did
briefly, under the broad sky
and the circling birds.

secret

A hundred years from Wilde
we choose secrecy with reluctance.
Even now, at the opening up
of a new century, a new millennium,
tolerance is tinged with prevarications,
those smiling hypocrisies
of the liberal conscience.

> (Do you remember
> that garish, painted statue
> of a reclining Wilde at the corner
> of Merrion Square?
> We cringed, and laughed together –
> but maybe he'd have appreciated
> its flamboyant wit…

> …except, of course, that you weren't there:
> shared holidays not risked, not yet; restricted
> to my imagined placing of you
> in every special, secret scene…)

What is a secret anyway?
An unseen connection,
a mutual knowing,
a glance, a look, a breath,
a dared half-smile across a crowded room.

couplets completed while you were away

Summer's last gasp of green sighs from the land,
Choked from the earth by Autumn's squeezing hand;
Tribal divisions crack the world apart,
Snaking their venom through the human heart;
Daily existence grinds its wearied way,
Aching to find some colour in the grey...

A nuthatch spotted, elegant and sleek,
Foraging insects with its probing beak;
A flash of brightness strikes its colours true
In shades of apricot and steely blue.

As Summer breathes again, despite the cold,
Alchemy's magic casts the land in gold;
And so my heart lifts, dreaming your return
And love's renewal as the seasons turn.

painting autumn for you

Autumn's dense riches
blaze gold outside my window.
The brush, poised midway in my skilless grip,
defers its choice of colour.
Perhaps words will do better
to brighten the painted landscape
in your quick imagination.

The lone magpie joins me again
in frail companionship.
It finds berries, a film of water
on the iced basin;
flaunts its oxymoronic plumage
in struts, stalkings and
dancing bursts of broken flight.
Its purposed thoughtfulness
renders me oddly pleased.

I think of your love,
anticipate your visit
with a lifting heart.
The brush chooses something bright,
greets the waiting paper with a kiss.

at christmas

Thoughts of you breathe warmth
into the air's chill,
streaking the windows' gathered condensation
to pooled absences.
Somewhere – your Dad's reluctant stand-in –
you carve the Christmas roast,
tender, for others whose love
demands your immediacy.
This makes me happy
when white laps frozen at doors and sills;
you're where you need to be,
pouring slow cream on
the fruited richness of pudding;
leading the cracker-pulling
that sparks laughing colours
through December's encroaching darkness.

Home alone,
I open your careful gifts,
hoping you'll find a quiet moment
to open mine,
and know that, best gift of all, you'll dare
to spare me a momentary thought
in the day's busyness.

world

Why do we still insist
on the world's not knowing?
Is it the twenty years between us
that make love awkward, unpermissible?
Or are we still unsure, unfixed,
a first draft, a preliminary sketch,
a tune half-recognised
amidst the world's white noise?

work in progress

The sky keeps its counsel.
Cracked jagged by winter's branched bareness,
it considers thin twigs, devoid of bud-bulge;
clogged earth, unsplit by spears of green;
fake Christmas brilliance wiped to white.
This is the nadir, snap and sap of spirit,
soul-shrunk January's pale wrap,
the squeeze and drain of residual hope...

...until anticipation lights
the dimmed horizon; until the thought of you
nourishes tomorrow, in sunset's soft flush
of pink and gold.

drive me

eased into place beside you
I relinquish control,
sure of your skill,
your expertise at the wheel;
happy to trust to your
shifting of gears, acceleration,
clutch-control and
brisk negotiation of
                    the quick road's sheer twist and drop –
                          switchback adrenaline dash
              through dreams' swift scenery –
                    startling lightscape of air-rush, star-fire and
                          breath's expansive, panting, exhilarating roar

the journey's a short one and
we end back where we started but –
the drive we've had!

nobody but you

you recognise in me
those haunted absences
that suck my spirit dry and drain the hope
from winter's shortening days

nobody knows but you
the damp, the drizzle and the dreariness
that shroud my soul
in guilt, regret and loss

perhaps you feel it too, but when we share
our momentary triumphs, aching dreams

you fill the absences,
brighten the fading hope,
dispel the dreariness, unshroud the soul
and gift the world with rainbows in the mist

another christmas

december, and the days draw darkness in,
shrinking light to a tight band,
a few dim hours
of damp grey

christmases, now, come thick and fast,
treading on one another's heels
with fake, insistent cheer
and fragile hope

hope, for us,
of times shared, brief hours
snatched from life's gaping roar,
moments together, rich in joy and love

unquestionable

that you should love me seems

impossible
in night's restless emptiness
when sleep washes its hands of me and
shifts me into the reaching of the dark

improbable
in the acid gaze of dawn
that sparks contempt in the cold eye
of the mirror's scrutiny

remarkable
in our talk's shared truths
tongued easy in the warmth
of words unspoken

unquestionable
in the folded peace of your soft touch
and the sun's golden kiss
on the covering sheets

fragile

Together we gather
White shells from the beach
And pass them like treasures
With care, each to each,
And know that we'll save them
For times when, apart,
We'll hear in their music
Heart beating to heart.

The sea's in their hollows,
Its breath and its scent,
And when we muse on them
We'll think what it meant
To be there together,
As when we're apart;
To pass them, with care,
Hand to hand, heart to heart.

lockdown love

Lockdown changed things –
too much, we thought at first,
for love to continue.
Our self-inflicted choice of secrecy, distance,
daring the thrill of moments together,
backfired into enforced separation,
days into months, made worse by
my technological backwardness: latter-day Luddite.
Skypeless, Zoomless, we texted, emailed,
shared precious calls until
your voice grew faint, your love, I feared, grew cold.

At last, restrictions eased, we met,
our distance confirmed by edict.
Obedient, fearful, we broke no rules;
you looked at me, I thought, as if
the wrong way through binoculars:
                diminished
                minimised
            cast into farness
        shrunk by the lack of you
Your new-grown beard
only inflamed my yearning:
your touch, your kiss, your body next to mine
and all the rest – forbidden.

But love pulled through; awkwardness
gave way to passion of a different kind,
voiced across empty spaces,
alive in eyes, in kindness and in smiles –
more than enough until the law allows
the touch of hands.
All's well, or will be:
we dared to love, we loved, we love, we will love.

Nothing will change; our world will be the same.

Confronting Art

Specimen

Interior with Mrs Mounter, Harold Gilman (1914-17)

Ashmolean Museum, Oxford

What do you see when, brush in hand,
you study my stout frame
in the door's space,
the day's tasks stilled,
pressed to the measure of your art's need?
What do you read in my stern look,
fixed, unnatural, under your
appraising gaze?

I am not Art, my apron
smudged with greased fingers,
mind bleared in the works
of the bright morning,
hazed with the ache
of war's long drift.
Can your paint show me
as I am to myself;
channel to the future
the pain of my slow days?

How will they read me, a century gone?
A footnote in your life's art:
drab, household moth
pinned to the smeared canvas.

The Disappeared

View of Scheveningen Sands with a Stranded Sperm Whale, Hendrick van Anthonissen (c. 1641)

Fitzwilliam Museum, Cambridge

Gathered in knots on the pale dunes,
For centuries they focused their blank gaze
On the waves' unremarkable swirling,
The mundane traffic of winter's wind-tossed white,
Blossom and billow of sail and surf and cloud.

And yet the channelled sightlines
Of these passive lookers-on
Must surely have posited an absence;
Or rather, a suppressed presence
Prisoned beneath the thickened paint.
Only now, picked flake by flake by
The restorer's patient scalpel
Is the spectacle unwrapped:
The beached whale's sad bulk
Dumped and slapped on the wet, flat sand.

Who chose to shift the artist's focus;
Airbrush the object of the gathered gaze
To nothingness;
To wipe the observer's thoughts, our thoughts,
Of wonder, amazement, disgust, compassion;
To neutralise the sea's thick stink
In collective amnesia?

The picture's history reaches for metaphor,
Aspires to allegory; make of it what you will.

Impossibilities

A Boy in an Orchard, Alfred Palmer (c. 1904)

Beaney House of Art and Knowledge, Canterbury

Distance, and turned backs.

The artist, it seems, imagines seasons' simultaneity:
Foregrounded trees, blossoming pale pink, contradict
Those further removed, silken with spring's green flush,
Where the girl reaches to pluck... what?
Emptiness only can fill her hand, her basket,
Unless we accept botanical impossibility.

Nearer, casual against the trunk's smoothed curve,
Basket brimming with impossible plums,
The boy leans, absorbed in texting... not her, I think.
This time, *my* impossibility:
I fix him a century ahead of Time,
Reading "now" into "then".
But if not texting, what
Absorbs his focused gaze, caressing hands?

Is it the painter's fault or mine
Interpretation falters?
Some lost or mislaid key
Frustrates elucidation,
Provokes wrong readings of the painted scene.

What's not in question, though:
- Separate together, they studiously avoid
  communication
- His furtive interest lies in something else
- Eden's lush orchard brought forth fruit, a serpent
- White hens, blood-crested, strut and peck, oblivious

72

Trompe l'oeil

Dining Room Mural, *Capriccio of a Mediterranean Seaport with British and Italian Buildings, the Mountains of Snowdonia, and a Self-Portrait Wielding a Broom*, Rex Whistler (1936-37)

Plas Newydd, Anglesey

He's painted himself into a corner.
                        Literally.
Broom in hand he contemplates, as we do,
his Italianate Snowdonian fantasy.
His magic sleights require no special glasses
but tug the eye beyond the painted wall –
a window speculation steps through
to unimagined depths and distances.
Who's round that corner? What lives proceed
in shuttered rooms? What thunders breed
in burgeoning clouds?

Gifting to the scene
crown, trident, damp footprints,
Neptune is visiting our world –
behind us perhaps in the Strait's kaleidoscopic
sparkle of mirrored mountains.
Abandoned too are spectacles, books,
the artist's left cigarette
wistfully smoking on the shaded step.
He'd be back to finish it, he joked:
one joke too many in Life's *trompe l'oeil*,
punchline twisted in war and death.
Inquisitive, speculative, the family dogs
investigate absences.
A cello with a broken string
scatters its music on the cold, grey stone.

Somewhere

The Goose Girl, Stanley Royle (c. 1921)

National Gallery of Ireland, Dublin

Night after night
we lead you to – somewhere.
In quiet dreams, dappled by morning,
you glide, tranced, through birches and bluebells,
upright, eyes fixed on a single purpose,
a promised destination, known but unseen.
In gown of orange and bonnet of white
you carry your gift of plucked blooms,
thick-juiced and drooping azure from the basket.
In your left hand, a birch-whip suggests control
of us, your goose-flock;
but *we* guide *you* through the speckled shade
and washes of light,
beyond the hopeful dream,
into the waking of another day.

I Am

Sunlight, Sir William Orpen (c. 1925)

National Gallery of Ireland, Dublin

Naked as I am
I am more than the object of / your prurient gaze.
The sunlight's morning wash
invests the room and me with clarity of purpose /
crisp as a cut apple.
I smooth the stocking sheer / along my leg
eager for the cool of its clinging.
The imminent day thrills / with possibilities
beyond your immediate painterly needs.
Why, though, is your precious Monet,
the Seine at Argenteuil,
given such prominence, such resonance /
above my profiled figure?
Do we both speak of light and space,
the calm peace of a scene so natural /
ordinary / touched with beauty?
We both are Art but I am
centre / focus / *raison d'être*
of your careful composition;
I live and breathe / have choices / agency /
here in this joyous cleansing of light;
I am not framed in heavy, sullen gold,
fixed to the wall to catch / your passing gaze.

Visions of War

Sandham Memorial Chapel, Stanley Spencer (1920s)

I'm lucky with the light that falls
Gently as fresh, clean sheets, soft on the dying.
It spreads its bright blessings from high windows
Into the chapel's dim mysteries,
Painting the walls with war's banal routines.
Laundry is sorted, lockers washed,
Beds made, floors scrubbed.
Crisped bacon, bread and jam, and urns of tea
Speak of a life that will and must go on
Somewhere outside these drab wards
Where war's scars penetrate beyond the flesh.

Far off, forgotten, you brave the Balkan front,
Its places named from your old Greek textbook
Of dusty conquests in a former time:
Macedonia, Salonika, Todorovo.
But you're behind the lines,
One set of mundane tasks swapped for another
In the dozing, midday heat between bitings of frost.
Kit checked, maps read, pits dug,
You wait to tend the as-yet-unwounded,
Whose unavoidable future plans its moment.

Rising behind the altar in the deep shade of the chapel's end,
Reality cracks:
War's dead burst from the clotted earth,
Awkwardly clamber through confusion
Of white crosses clustering thick in tangled heaps.
Each soldier, born again,
Bears his death's marker, like the crucified,
Far across the receding, discoloured
Landscape of bleared browns, to lay at the feet
Of a distant, receiving Christ.

These paintings speak
With childish innocence and an adult's knowing
To us, across a ravaged century.
Visionary, poignant,
They flood the eyes with unexpected tears.

Spring Mourning

The Boer War 1900-01, John Byam Liston Shaw
(1901)

> "Oh last summer green things were greener,
> Brambles fewer, the blue sky bluer!"
> > Christina Rossetti, "A Bird Song"

Birmingham Museum and Art Gallery

When he left I didn't imagine
the possibility of loss.
Half a world away he nobly fought
some imprecisely-articulated enemy,
some dark foe, easily vanquished
with the flash of a sabre in the burning sun.
He'd come back with a scar, perhaps,
with skin bronzed tough as the dry plains
of an unknown continent.
At home I read, and sewed,
played Chopin, danced, penned cheerful letters,
crafted my trivia to a journal,
social *minutiae* to share on his return.

Now, etched in ebony, I stand
in spring's renewing green.
Grief ripples dark in the water,
flaps black in the raven's ragged flight.
Briefly I contemplate Ophelia,
weave garlands from willow-herb, loosestrife,
purples and pinks to match the skein of thread
that hangs, grief's talisman, loosely from my hand.
Vacant, absent, I ache to imagine
that vast, parched plain
stained with the purple of his spent blood.

Showstopper

The Great British Bake Off

Can I call it Art?
– this eclectic confection of
flour / butter / sugar / cream
pastry / dough / savoury / sweet
cake / pie / loaf / bun
competition / innuendo
judgment / dismissal
disaster & tears & (sometimes) blood

and kindness, always kindness –
the yeast that raises,
proves the spirit,
swells to readiness
the bake of friendship.

Love is dispensable,
we can live without it;
kindness the jam and cream
holding together
our showstopping Victoria sponge.

That Love

Selected Poems, Kate Clanchy (2014)

Your poems, a birthday gift,
draw my grudging admiration
for their way of looking:
sharp, precise, askew.

Those at the end –
"Newborn" you called them –
ache with that specific, that particular
vivid, visceral,
uncompromising love.
They loosen something in me:
unease, embarrassment at
all that baby stuff,
that wonder in the knowing
that you had made this magic thing,
this questing, fragile hope.

Quickly I skim each one,
pass over them, mind half closed,
pretend they're sentimental, twee,
not to my taste –

but my eyes sting
knowing I
have never had
can never have
that love

Spirits of Time

Three ghost stories

"Remember me when I am gone away,
Gone far away into the silent land;
When you can no more hold me by the hand,
Nor I half turn to go, yet turning stay."

Christina Rossetti, "Remember"

"With a smile on her lips and a tear in her eye."

Sir Walter Scott, *Marmion*

"O, Antony!"

William Shakespeare, *Antony and Cleopatra*

Quando verrà il momento

Evelyn had been waiting months for Roberto to invite her back to his home, but now she was here she was beginning to wish she hadn't come. Standing alone in his room, in the flickering light of a dozen candles, she found the dense summer heat increasingly oppressive. The dregs of the Italian sunset pressed their feeble glow against the blinds, and the thick, warm scent of lavender and rosemary filled her head. She listened indifferently to the bursts of rough coughing coming from the bathroom, where he'd gone to take his evening medication. For the first time, she wondered if she was right to think she loved him; maybe she was just under his spell.

As the shadows played teasingly on the walls, her mind returned to the question of who had lit the candles. Rationally, she knew it must be the housekeeper, whose pale face she thought she'd glimpsed in an upper window when they'd arrived. However, she was more concerned with the two photographs that stood side by side on the dressing table. On the left was a young man in uniform, sporting a rifle over his shoulder and a jaunty smile; on the right, a middle-aged woman in traditional peasant dress, facing the camera with a stern, unforgiving expression. The soldier was recognisably Roberto, looking much younger than he did now; the woman, she assumed, was his mother – or perhaps his grandmother. He'd once told her, half laughing, that he was from good peasant stock, and proud of it. Why, though, did she find the photographs so unsettling?

Just over an hour ago, when they'd left the city, she'd been in a state of pleasurable excitement. The drive out of the stifling suburbs up into the foothills in his open-topped, silver Mercedes, was like the most perfect dream.

Closing her eyes, she imagined the hillsides carved into slick curves by their accelerating ascent. The roadside pines breathed their incense into the warm rush of air that caressed her tingling skin; this was how he would touch her as they lay together on his bed, windows open to the stars, absorbing the distant stirrings of the sea.

When they'd arrived, the house was just as she'd pictured it, an elegant villa fronted by a colonnade bathed in the rosy glow of the departing sun. So vivid was it that she almost thought she'd seen it before, in a photograph album perhaps. The only jarring note was the half-glimpsed face at the high window, spoiling her vision of their own, private paradise. The car crunched to a halt on the gravel drive and he turned off the engine. At first there was silence, until her ears refocused on the competing choruses of insect chirping and vibrant birdsong, filling the evening with celebration of another day survived.

He led her to the front door, tucked into the soft shade of the columned portico, and told her to turn round. She did so, and the world opened out before her in a steep tumbling away of trees and shadows under the crimson sunset. On either side, the purple mountains lifted their heads towards the stars, shading into the sky's deepening indigo. Directly ahead, the Mediterranean's enigmatic expanse glittered and sparkled in silver and red.

"Well," said Roberto. "What do you think?"

"It's lovely," she replied, not knowing what else to say, even in English. She wished, as usual, that she had a quicker mind, a richer vocabulary, a sharper emotional intelligence. He was bound to tire of her before long.

As they entered the dark house she recalled her surprise when, earlier that day, he'd asked her if she'd like to go back there with him. Previously, he'd seemed defensive, reluctant to admit her to the intimacies of his private existence. His mother had died last year, just before they'd started seeing each other, and she could understand why he might find it difficult to take her back to his family home. She was pleased, though, that he'd changed his mind; perhaps after all she was wrong to think he had reservations about their relationship.

Even so, she knew she wasn't clever enough for him. What could he possibly see in her: this pale, reserved English girl who was always asking dumb questions in his classes? Still, at least her Italian was improving, and sometimes they managed to sustain brief conversations in his language rather than hers. She preferred it, though, when he spoke in English, his rich Neapolitan accent infusing the familiar words with passionate intensity.

She tried not to think of the gaps that lay between them, in age, cultural background and experience. When the war ended, ten years ago now, she was still a child, but he would have been old enough to take part in those dying days of chaos and disintegration. She'd never asked him about it but she hoped, with her usual romantic idealism, that he'd been a resistance fighter, a member of the *partigiani* who had stood up against Mussolini's fascist regime. She knew about them because her father had been one of the British troops assigned to support them in their struggle.

Now, though, she was looking at a photograph of Roberto in Italian army uniform, swelling with pride in his smart military outfit. Could he really have been one of the people her father had fought against? Before he had died out here – or, at least, been reported "missing, presumed dead" – her father had developed a love for Italy and its people which had inspired her to come here to study, despite her mother's puzzling opposition. But perhaps she was being too hard on Roberto; after all, she was only looking at a photograph of a young man who had fought for his country. Who could blame him for that?

Idly, she picked up the photograph and turned it over, but there was nothing on the back. She did the same with the picture of the woman and could just make out, in the flickering dimness, a scrawled inscription: "*Quando verrà il momento, io ci sarò,*" followed by the name Giorgio. Even her limited Italian could cope with this: "When the time comes, I'll be there." At first, she found it comforting, reassuring, until she realised with a start that it could also be interpreted as a threat. And who was Giorgio? Hearing Roberto's footsteps in the corridor, she hastily replaced the photograph in its place. His firm voice interrupted her confused reflections.

"I'm sorry," he said. "Perhaps I shouldn't have brought you here." More quietly, he added, "*Espiazione.*"

She turned to confront him but, not for the first time, was thrown off balance by the magnetism of his physical presence.

"Are you feeling better?" she asked weakly.

He was stripped to the waist, and she gazed appreciatively at his smooth, firm beauty. Her eyes were drawn, as they always were, to the faint, roughly-healed scar on the right side of his chest, just above his ribs. Her searching fingers, too, always lingered there, fascinated by its mystery, which she knew she would never dare ask him to explain. Nor would she ask him about that final, whispered word. She had heard it before, during the Catholic services he sometimes took her to, and it hadn't been difficult to work out what it meant. *Espiazione*: expiation, atonement.

All her uncertainties evaporated in the gentle thrill of their lovemaking, which instantly transported her to the paradise she had imagined. She felt absorbed into his existence in a way she never had in the noisy heat of the city. Afterwards, she fell into a deep, relaxing sleep, only half-conscious of his irregular breathing. From time to time, as usual, she was aware of a sudden, convulsive shift in his position, accompanied by whispered fragments of speech. She was used to this, and it had long ago ceased to trouble her. Often, to her surprise, her semi-conscious mind heard his incoherent ramblings half in English, even though he spoke in Italian. "OK, *va bene*," he muttered at one point. "It's all right – I needed her to be here." Without even wondering what his words meant, she drifted back into a calm and dreamless sleep.

In the morning, she woke before him and lay still for a while, watching the shadows fluttering on the pale walls and trembling in faint webs across the disarranged sheets. The dawn chorus was building to an optimistic crescendo and she could almost hear the sea's distant throb. Only one candle was still alight, its diminished flame spluttering vainly in the face of imminent extinction.

She must have dozed off again, though she felt wide awake and totally alert. Outside, voices were shouting urgently, barking curses and commands into the echoing air. Feet crunched on the gravel drive and bursts of gunfire grew steadily closer, mingled with screams of anger and pain. The wind roared and howled, and she imagined a blizzard, a swirling inferno of fiery, white destruction. A shrill voice called out, "*Traditore!*" before being silenced by a single shot.

Quickly, she rose from the bed, stepped over to the window, opened the blinds and looked out. Everything was quiet. The view he'd shown her so proudly when they'd arrived stretched out under bright, grey skies to the calm of the Mediterranean, shimmering with promise in the pale morning light. As she pulled her gaze back to the edge of the drive, in the shadows cast by the towering pines, she thought she could make out the figure of a man staring intently up at the house. He reminded her oddly of her father. She rubbed her eyes and looked again, but there was no-one there.

Turning into the room, she reached for the silk dressing-gown Roberto had lent her, which she'd left draped over the bedside chair. She listened for a moment to his breathing, calm and regular for once, and cast her eyes over his sleeping form, wrapped loosely in the tangled sheets. She thought how little she knew about him. Did it matter? He was clever, that much was certain; as his student she was in awe of him. As his lover, though, she adored his contradictions. He was romantic and practical; reserved and eloquent; aloof and attentive. Yet no-one, she thought, could be more gentle, more considerate; never before had she been with someone who made her so happy. Dismissing the fleeting remnants of her unnerving dream, she laughed lightly to herself and padded out in search of the bathroom.

When she came back, she knew at once that something had changed. The last candle had gone out, leaving a thin plume of smoke ascending in dark ripples towards the ceiling. She felt oppressed by a sense of absence and realised that the birds' bright singing had stopped, leaving a palpable vacancy of sound. With a jolt of anxiety she crossed to the bed. Roberto was lying there, unnaturally still, neatly arranged on his back with the covers smoothed and pulled up to his chest, and he was not breathing. She couldn't take it in, couldn't think what to do.

It took her a few minutes to notice that his photograph had been replaced in its frame by another: a man dressed in the improvised uniform of the Italian resistance, rifle at the ready. She looked at it more closely. There was no doubt about it: it was her father.

Behind her, someone cleared their throat. She turned in fear. Standing in the doorway, arms linked in mutual affection, were her father and the woman from the other photograph.

Her father, George – Giorgio.

He smiled at her, sadly. "Evelyn," he said.

End of Days

It was the strangest of days. A hazy, ochre light filled the air, as if the New Forest's October leaves had squeezed all their yellows and golds into a sickly infusion. As the little ferry chugged steadily across the marina, weaving smoothly through the stilled yachts, it was possible to look directly at the sun, reduced by the day's sulphurous veil to a bright copper disc. For once, nobody spoke. Mary, usually so full of good cheer, looked as if she'd just received sad news. Even Kieron, the ferryman, seemed subdued, his attention focused on the squat outline of Hurst Castle ahead of them, flattened like an enormous crab on its raised promontory. Jack found the silence unnerving, but didn't want to be the one to break it.

The morning's news had been full of speculation about the unusual atmospheric conditions, which had dimmed daylight and shrunk the spectrum to this eerie yellow filter. The internet was rife with end-of-days scenarios, substituting superstition for science.

As they approached the Castle, Jack felt increasingly anxious. He remembered the first time he'd come here, just after the war. He and his Aunt Emily had tramped along the spit from Milford-on-Sea, crunching the shingle into irregular hollows. The Castle was still occupied then, by a skeleton-staff who kept it ticking over for a re-mobilisation that never materialised. As a local girl, Emily had performed here with Betty Hockey's troupe of Nonstops, whose high-kicking routines had spiced up the wartime variety shows at the Garrison Theatre. Jack still had the framed sepia photograph of her, smiling at the theatre door. She wasn't really his aunt; a city boy, he'd been evacuated to the New Forest to live with her family. Here he discovered fresh air, open countryside and the sharp press of the sea breeze on his raw skin. They were all dead now, all ghosts; and he was old.

When the boat had moored at the wooden jetty, Jack let the others get off first: Mary with her bunch of rusty keys, ready to unlock the Castle for the day's visitors; young Ian, the café manager, with his assistant Jamila; and two of the workmen engaged in the restoration work on the west wing. None of them spoke, either to him or to each other; all seemed weighed down by the dreary light, curdling now into a syrupy gloom like the prelude to an eclipse. Perhaps the doom-sayers were right after all.

Stepping on to the sallow turf, Jack felt uneasy; he was relieved, though, that at least he hadn't been coughing this morning. It was Emily, he recalled, who'd given him his first cigarette.

"See you later," he said to Kieron, and added, "Strange day."

The ferryman barely glanced at him as he cast off and brought the boat round to return to Keyhaven. Jack loved this name: the place where the keys to the Castle were cherished and kept safe.

When Jack retired from his job on the railways, he'd moved back to Milford and offered his services as a volunteer at the Castle. As resident handyman, he soon established himself as an indispensable part of the team. He steeped himself in the Castle's characters and stories, which he would happily embroider for the benefit of visiting children. He particularly relished tales of the theatre, such as the moonless night when his aunt and her companions were almost stranded at the Castle after drinks in the officers' mess. They had to be carried out to their drifting boat by two or three soldiers in pitch darkness and thrown into it before it retreated on the receding tide.

As Jack passed through the dark gateway into the grass-hummocked courtyard, he thought he heard voices whispering his name. This was not unusual; for ages now he had felt in tune with the spirits of those who had lived and died here. After dumping his work-bag in the big shed where the maintenance staff were based, he began his day, as he always did, on the roof of Henry VIII's circular fort, breathing in the spectacular view. Today, though, it was unearthly and disturbing under the sky's thickening yellow, and he felt suddenly afraid. The Castle's Victorian extensions stretched out each way along the promontory, enclosing the bleak salt-marshes in the crab's reaching pincers. A little way along the shingle spit, a couple laboured towards the Castle with a small child. The Isle of Wight was a formless haze, penetrated only by the regular blink of the Needles light. The upper air, turbulent now, twisted jaundiced leaves from far inland into a spinning vortex, shrill with the voices of the Castle's dead. And from the Garrison Theatre's scooped-out cave of an auditorium, tucked away in the redbrick, Victorian west wing, Jack could hear the sound of cheerful music and raucous laughter reverberating through the dense air.

Assuming the Castle's sound-system had malfunctioned, Jack hurried down the spiralling stone steps back towards the theatre. This was where his aunt and her troupe had joked, sung and danced away the war, one night at a time, for hundreds of servicemen with no expectation of living longer than a few weeks. He could smell the acrid tang of packed bodies, the fug of cigarette smoke and stale beer, and as a thrill of fear trembled through his body, the air's nicotine-stained fingers closed around him.

He was distracted by the arrival of the day's first visitors, the family he'd seen negotiating the shingle bank. This, surely, would restore normality; he would entertain

91

them with some of the Castle's livelier stories, like the Nonstops and their vanishing boat. The little girl ran towards him across the tussocky grass, as if she sensed he had tales to tell. He knew she was going to trip even before she went flying and sprawled headlong in front of him. He braced himself to catch her, but to his horror she tumbled straight through him, as if she were merely an insubstantial projection of the sulphurous light.

The music rose into a head-spinning cacophony. The girl started crying as her parents rushed towards her and lifted her gently to her feet. Jack turned away, cursing his stupidity, understanding everything: for him, it was the end of days. At the theatre entrance, suffused in sepia twilight, Aunt Emily gave him a welcoming smile. Relaxing, he smiled back.

Haunting

There was absolutely no doubt in Frank's mind that when he'd woken up that morning he'd been in his own house. He distinctly remembered drawing back the curtains in his upstairs bedroom and looking out at the narrow strip of garden, with its neatly mown lawn and tidy spring borders, stretching towards the scrappy allotments that were just visible through the bare hedge he'd planted to establish the family's privacy. Somewhere over there, a few years ago, a retreating German bomber had dropped the last of its load after a raid on Birmingham's industrial heartland. The blast had blown the clock off their mantelpiece and sent them scurrying, in the early evening gloom, to the improvised shelter he'd dug in what had been his wife's treasured vegetable patch. At least the war was over now and, with a bit of luck, there'd never be another one. But then, the previous war had been mistakenly passed off as "the war to end war", hadn't it?

Feeling inexplicably weary, his joints stiff and aching, he'd gone back to bed for a while, listening to the sound of his wife busy downstairs in the kitchen. For a moment he forgot her name as he dozed, but it instantly came back to him, of course. Muriel. She was his rock, his support in times of trouble – though when he'd been away from her at the war's end, clearing up the wreckage as he'd thought of it, he was aware that something had changed between them. *She* was the same, but he wasn't; the things he'd seen made him a different person. Even now – what was it, six, seven years later? – he was aware that he'd blocked out some of the more distressing images from his time in Italy and North Africa. Yet he knew too that his experiences there had also been an awakening, an opening up of potentialities in his life that had crumpled, and crumbled, on his return to the same old job in the same old place with – he guiltily acknowledged – the same old wife. He loved her, he thought, though they no longer slept together; he certainly loved the boys. Barry was now seven, or was it eight? And David was just two. They were the reason he stayed; they would live the lives that had been denied to him.

He decided he'd been lying there long enough. It must be 9.00 by now, he thought. He supposed it was Saturday or Sunday, otherwise he'd already be at work. Even at weekends, though, he was invariably up first; there were always jobs to be done while Muriel was getting the breakfast: the car to be checked over, the lawn to be cut, tools to be tidied and rearranged in the shed he'd built when they moved in, just before the war started. Men's jobs.

Opening his eyes, he'd known immediately that something was wrong. There was an atmosphere about the room: the quality of the light, perhaps, or maybe a scent, or an unfamiliar sound that brought to mind the distant throbbing of the sea. Though he knew he'd left the curtains open when he'd got up earlier, they were closed now. His wife must have closed them. Muriel. Yet surely he would have been aware of her coming in; after all, he hadn't been asleep, merely dozing. He pushed himself up into a sitting position and winced as a twinge of pain shot into his back. Blinking the remnants of sleep from his eyes, he glanced round the room. He didn't recognise it. Pushing back the bedclothes, he swivelled round to get out on the left side of the bed as usual and realised with a surge of panic that the door had gone. Where was he? He forced himself to his feet, feeling frail and somehow insubstantial, and looked round the room again. There was the door – on the wrong side of the bed! Was this Alice's looking-glass world? He'd read the story so many times to his eldest son. Barry, that was it. The room was certainly hauntingly familiar – but it wasn't right! Perhaps he was still half-asleep. The window, with its unfamiliar, floral curtains, would solve the mystery. He shuffled towards it; at least it was where it should be, opposite the foot of his bed. He drew apart the curtains and stared.

His heart pounded and his head ached as he tried to make sense of what he saw. Instead of their tiny, narrow suburban garden, he was looking out at a low-walled patch of scrubby grass that vanished into a shifting white fog, through which he could make out fluctuating glimpses of an incomprehensible seascape. Fading in and out of visibility, the sea was a choppy, steely, glittering expanse of tossed waves, peaked with foamy flecks of white. Jagged, threatening rocks crashed the heaving water into unpredictable fountains of spray, vanishing and reappearing as the wind swirled the mist into dim, rearranged vistas. And far away, barely perceptible against the pale blankness of the sky, a thin strip of grey land marked the horizon, disappearing and reappearing as he tried to blink away his puzzlement and panic.

Frank sat down heavily at the foot of his bed and tried to think. In a moment of clarity, he knew what was happening. This was one of those dreams – those intense, vivid, oppressive dreams where you know you're dreaming and desperately want to wake up, but can't. Then, finally, you do wake up, to a sense of unutterable relief. Everything around you is more or less as it should be – but you can't move and you realise you're still dreaming and everything's wrong and strange again and so it goes on and on until finally you wake up for real. Clearly he hadn't yet reached that point.

He forced himself to sit upright, placed his hands on his pyjamaed knees and began to breathe as regularly as he could to still the beating panic. In the dream, he noticed, his hands were knobbly, and wrinkled, and old. How old was he, actually? Thirty-eight? Forty? Something like that. A voice spoke quietly from behind him, from the door – the door that was on the *wrong side* of his bed!

"You're up."

Was it Muriel's voice? He thought it was, but he daren't look. The dream would end soon, then it would be all right. There was no point trying to rush it.

"Are you ready for some breakfast?"

It sounded like her, he thought – almost. He turned to look at her and his heart jumped as he saw an old woman, her face pale and wrinkled, hair lightly permed, an uncertain smile hidden in her eyes and mouth. She spoke again.

"Are you OK? You don't need to get up yet. David won't be here for another hour; the Scillonian doesn't get in till 12.30."

Frank felt panic and anger rising inside him. "Who are you?" he said. "Where is this? Where's Muriel?"

Her face became hard, her eyes cold. He sensed he'd said something wrong, that she was disappointed, as angry with him as he was with her, whoever she was.

"Frank," she said, conjuring a voice as sympathetic as she could manage. "We're at home. On Tresco. Don't you recognise it? Me?"

"Tresco? What's that?"

"The Isles of Scilly. Where we used to come on holiday – surely you remember – before we were married? It was my aunt's cottage then. Then we moved here when you retired." She paused, then muttered, half to herself, "Big mistake."

He did remember, something. On holiday. Rugged cliffs and crashing waves. Long beaches as white as marble. Swathes of bluebells and wild garlic, and those bright, startling, exotic blooms growing lush across the island landscapes. Was that where he was now? He couldn't work it out, and wouldn't try. No, he *wouldn't*.

"Get out," he said. "Leave me alone. I want Muriel."

"For heaven's sake, Frank, Muriel's – never mind." She sighed – a sigh of frustration, of accusation. "I'll go and get your breakfast," she said tightly. "Tea and toast, all right." It wasn't a question.

The door closed behind her with unnecessary force, and Frank felt inexplicably sorry. He knew now that he was awake, but that just made things worse. Who was that woman, for God's sake? And did she say David was coming? What David? Not his son, he was only two. Who could be bringing him?

The door opened again and the old woman who wasn't Muriel reappeared. "Here," she said, her voice soft with apology. "Maybe this will remind you."

She placed a large, framed photograph carefully on the bed, smiled sadly at him and went out again, closing the door with barely a sound.

Despite his growing sense of apprehension, Frank picked up the photograph and gave it a perfunctory glance, but he could make nothing of it. Tossing it angrily back on the eiderdown, he remained seated on the edge of the bed, hardly aware that he was beginning to feel uncomfortably cold.

☆   ☆   ☆   ☆   ☆

When the strange woman returned, Frank felt much calmer. She called softly from outside the door, "Breakfast," then came in with his tea and toast on a tray. Perhaps she's a ghost, he thought vaguely.

"You're still up," she said with a frown. "You must be getting chilly. Here, let me get you back into bed."

She picked up the framed photograph and put it on top of a chest of drawers behind the door, then helped to negotiate him through his twinges of pain into a sitting position in bed, propped up against the pillows. She pulled the covers over him, smoothed them out and placed the tray and its contents carefully in front of him. Whoever she was, she seemed kind, he thought. A kind ghost.

The toast was just as he liked it, spread thickly with chunky marmalade. "Thank you," he forced himself to say; then, irrelevantly, "I'm old."

"Yes," she replied. "You and me both." She sat down heavily on the small armchair in the corner of the room by the window.

"What's your name?"

She resisted the urge to answer crossly. "It's Catherine, Frank. Your wife."

He began to panic. His wife, he knew, was called Muriel. That couldn't be wrong. But before he could object, correct her, she went on, "Don't you remember? Everyone called me Cathy, which I hated, except you. You said my name was too special to be shortened."

"Catherine." Though it seemed familiar, he still struggled to make sense of it, feeling the name on his tongue, the vibrations it made, as if that would somehow unlock his understanding. "But Muriel is my wife," he said stubbornly.

She knew the best thing to do would be to give in, say she was Muriel, not try to contradict him in his heightened state of anxiety. But that would be to betray herself, to betray the life they'd had together. It was pointless, she knew, but she was desperate to convince him of everything they'd shared over the past twenty years. She

98

had never even known Muriel, had only met Frank in 1973, three years after that terrible accident, when he was still raw from the loss; raw not so much because of the love he still felt for his late wife as for the knowledge that their marriage had been on the point of disintegration when she stormed off to return to her parents in the north-east. There had been an appalling pile-up on the M1…

Frank had finished his breakfast and was staring blankly at the crumbed plate. He picked up his cup for a final sip of tea, realised it was empty and put it back down.

"Where are we?" he said.

"Tresco, Frank. In the Isles of Scilly. This is where we fell in love – with each other and with the islands," she added wistfully.

"Scilly," he repeated blankly. The word failed to resonate in his mind.

"Yes, Frank," she said. "You don't remember," she added, her voice weary, defeated.

For a moment there was silence: an absence, an emptiness.

Then, "When is it?" he said.

She was puzzled. "What do you mean?"

He couldn't get his thoughts clear; couldn't explain what he wanted to know.

"When is it? Now. What is it – what year – date? When are we now?"

She could sense the frustration, the panic, welling up inside him, and she felt intensely sorry for him. But whenever she tried to explain the truth to him, she regretted it. The incomprehension, the impossibilities, made him angry, and he still possessed an unexpected physical strength that could fly out at random, knock things over, break things. One day, she thought, he would lash out, hit her, and the whole thing would be finished. Always, though, she held on to the hope that he would understand, accept the truth – remember everything.

"It's 1995, Frank. November."

He didn't reply, didn't react at all. Then he said, apparently irrelevantly, "Where are the boys?"

The boys, she thought; his and Muriel's boys. David would be here shortly, if the Scillonian arrived at St Mary's on time. As for Barry, six years older, he'd never reconciled himself to his father's new relationship nor come to terms with the loss of his mother. This was one truth Catherine had no wish to force into Frank's oblivious mind. It was unlikely to arise, though, when David arrived, as Frank would not accept this balding, middle-aged man as his younger son, and David was sensible – and sensitive – enough not to make an issue of it, so there would be no awkward questions. David's role was to be the friendly visitor and he played it with cheerful conviction, whatever his real feelings might be. But then, Catherine thought bitterly, he could afford the privilege of emotional neutrality: he only visited once a year, when he stayed on the neighbouring island of Bryher.

Ignoring Frank's question, Catherine stood up and went over to the chest of drawers.

"Did you look at this?" she said, picking up the photograph. "Here," she added, passing it across to him, "do you remember it?"

He took the picture, looked at it and saw a couple in late middle-age, warmly and cosily dressed despite the blue skies and the sharp shadows cast by the sun. They were sitting side by side on a rocky outcrop, amidst clumps of bright yellow gorse, looking out across a narrow channel towards a small island.

Frank said nothing for a while, but studied the photograph intently. Then, in one of those random, surprising moments of clarity that made her feel struggling on with him was worthwhile, he asked, "Is it us?"

"Yes," she said, "it's us. It was our first time here after we got married."

"Oh," he said; then, astutely, "Who took it – the picture?"

"Clive did – don't you remember? We bumped into him while we were walking along the cliffs and he offered to take a photo of us together." She laughed, feeling the moment – twenty years ago – as vividly as if it had just happened. Almost to herself, she said, "We were so in love that we were a bit embarrassed, typically English. We couldn't look at each other, or even at the camera. It would reveal too much…"

"Clive… I know him, don't I?"

"Yes," she said excitedly, her heart lifting as it did every time he showed the slightest sign of remembering something. "He worked at the Abbey Gardens. Then when we retired here a few years later you volunteered there as an assistant gardener. He was your boss."

She stopped suddenly, wishing she hadn't mentioned Clive; painfully aware that the past wasn't as simple, as clear-cut, as her re-editing of it for the benefit of the husband she had once loved. For a time – a short time she always convinced herself – Clive had been a complication.

She became aware that Frank was looking at her intently, and felt her cheeks flush – but not, surely, with guilt or shame? It was only after Frank had begun to forget things, when Clive had been so thoughtful and under-standing, that something had happened between them. But it hadn't lasted, she told herself; not on her side, at least.

She stood up, trying not to look flustered. "Let me take those things," she said.

She sensed suddenly that Frank had gone from her, that his mind was already somewhere else, forty or fifty years away, perhaps; somewhere she could never join him. In a flash of realisation she knew he wouldn't be with her for much longer – unless, she reflected, half seriously, he should come back to haunt her. When he was dead, she wondered, would he know everything – about her and Clive? If his ghost did indeed return, though, it would be nothing new; after all, he had, effectively, been his own ghost for a long time.

Unexpectedly, as she reached to pick up his tray, he put his hand on hers and smiled up at her.

"Catherine," he said.

*   *   *   *   *

Frank looked out across the narrow garden towards the allotments. Downstairs, Muriel was busy in the kitchen; he could hear her clattering about as usual, and hoped she wouldn't be in one of her silent moods. He knew things weren't the same between them, probably never would be. He'd been back for six years, or was it seven? In all that time, he'd said nothing to her, or to anyone else for that matter, about those dregs of the war that had taken away the last years of his youth and plunged him into middle age. The country was full of hope – rebuilding, renewal, a young Queen – yet he felt, somehow, he'd missed the boat. It was only the boys that kept him going; they deserved better than he'd had. They deserved something that had always eluded him, something he should have enjoyed with Muriel, but never did. They deserved love.

Annoyed with himself, he shook off his gloomy reflections and checked his appearance in the mirror. He wasn't bad looking, he thought, and was smartly turned out – as he always tried to be, even at weekends. If Muriel couldn't love him, she could at least be proud of him. But there was a hesitancy in him this morning, an unwillingness to face her. When he went into the kitchen and gave her a smile and a kiss, he knew he would feel even more of a fraud than usual.

He frowned. What was wrong with him, he wondered? He was half aware of the shredded remnants of a dream flickering and fading in his head. Unfamiliar scenes, a half-recognised face, a sense of being old before his time. But he couldn't cling on to them, couldn't construct them into anything coherent. As he touched the door handle, ready to walk out into whatever the day had in store, he was aware of a quiet voice, faintly calling his name.

"Frank," it said, "do you remember? Can you hear me?"

He turned round, but there was no-one there. How could there be? He saw cliffs, a white beach and sparkling surf; bluebells, wild garlic and bright, exotic blooms. Was he still asleep? Was this one of those dreams that tricks you into thinking you've woken up? He thought he heard a name, familiar but uncertain, and sensed something that made him frown – a betrayal, perhaps.

"Are you there, Frank?" asked the voice, melting into the gentle fall of the waves. "Do you remember?"

"Catherine?" he said

Notes

At virtually every poetry event or "open mic" session where I have read my work, there has been one frustrating rule: no introductions, just read the poem! Of course a poem should stand by itself without the need for superfluous explanation; but poetry is difficult, particularly at first reading or first hearing, so sometimes a brief context can provide a helpful way in for the reader or listener. With that in mind, I have provided these short notes on some of the poems; further information on the places and people celebrated in the book can of course be found on the internet.

Queen of Crime (p. 6)

Greenway was the holiday home of Agatha Christie from 1938. It inspired a number of her novels including *Dead Man's Folly* (1956), in which the body of the first victim is discovered in the boathouse. Much of the 2013 TV adaptation starring David Suchet as Hercule Poirot was filmed there.

Machine for Living (p. 7)

High Cross House, which was briefly in the care of the National Trust, was built in the 1930s modernist style for William Curry, the headmaster of Dartington Hall School. The phrase "machine for living" was a catch-phrase at the time for this architectural style.

The Melancholy Walk (p. 8)

The Melancholy Walk runs through the grounds of Saltram House, near Plymouth, which are bounded on the west by the River Plym and on the north by the A38.

The D'Oyly Cartes (p. 9)

Coleton Fishacre, an Arts and Crafts/Art Deco-style house, was built in the 1920s for Rupert and Lady Dorothy D'Oyly Carte. Their son Michael was killed in a car crash in Switzerland in 1932 at the age of 21, an event that split up the family.

Hoard (p. 10)

Overbeck's is named after its former owner, the eccentric collector and inventor Otto Overbeck, and is home to an old-fashioned and eclectic museum. Its gardens command fine views over the Salcombe estuary.

Drake at Home (p. 11)

Buckland Abbey was founded in 1278. Sir Francis Drake lived there from about 1581, after his circumnavigation of the globe, until his death in 1596 – a period during which he was second-in-command of the English fleet that defeated the Spanish Armada in 1588. The buildings were badly damaged by fire in 1938.

Post-Prandial (p. 13)

Stowe's Temple of Friendship was built by Lord Cobham in 1739 to entertain his political friends and allies. Facing it across the valley, the Queen's Temple – also known as the Lady's Temple or the Temple of Female Friendship – was where Lady Cobham hosted her own social gatherings.

Sourcing Shakespeare: *He that killed the deer* (p. 16)

Charlecote was the home of the Lucy family, whose coat-of-arms included three pike ("luce" in old French). Legend has it that the young Shakespeare was caught poaching deer in the park and brought before Sir Thomas Lucy, who was the local magistrate – and that the playwright had his revenge by caricaturing Sir Thomas as Justice Shallow in *The Merry Wives of Windsor* and *Henry IV Part 2*.

Sourcing Shakespeare: *Refuge* (p. 17)

Shakespeare must surely have known Baddesley Clinton, a moated manor-house probably dating from the 13th century, which would have been the perfect setting for Mariana's "moated grange" in *Measure for Measure* – and even more so Tennyson's poem "Mariana". Its tenant, Anne Vaux, gave refuge to fugitive Catholic priests; the Jesuit, Father Henry Garnet, lived there for over 13 years and may have helped to create the so-called "priest-holes" hidden within the fabric of the house.

In a 1591 raid by the authorities, Garnet and others were concealed in these, having fled their beds and turned over their mattresses so it was less obvious they'd been sleeping there. Garnet was tried and executed in 1606 for his alleged part in the Gunpowder Plot. At his trial he defended himself using the notorious technique of equivocation, and is probably the "equivocator" referred to by the Porter in *Macbeth*, written later the same year.

Home Guard (p. 18)

This poem is based on photographs on display at the Courts Garden. The house and garden were purchased by Major Clarence Goff in 1921. He had served in the Second Boer War of 1900-02 and in the Great War; during World War Two he commanded the local Home Guard unit, which sometimes met in the garden. He and his wife, Lady Cecilie, were visited at the Courts by Queen Mary. *Bargello* is a type of needlepoint embroidery named after that found on patterned chairs in Florence's Bargello Palace.

Scriptorium Vitae (p. 19)

Sissinghurst was the home of the diplomat, writer and politician Harold Nicolson and his wife Vita Sackville-West, whose writing-room was in the tower and who famously had affairs with Violet Trefusis and Virginia Woolf. "*Vita*", of course, is Latin for "life".

White Cliffs: *Ancestral voices* (p. 22)

During the Battle of Britain in 1940 a German Dornier 17 was shot down and crashed into the English Channel

Eloi and Morlocks (p. 23)

H. G. Wells's mother became housekeeper at Uppark in 1880, having previously worked there as a lady's maid. Wells stayed there often in his youth, and the extensive servants' tunnels almost certainly influenced his social ideas, most strikingly in the dystopian future he envisaged in *The Time Machine*.

Ellen Terry as Lady Macbeth (p. 24)

Ellen Terry's dress for Henry Irving's 1888-89 production of *Macbeth*, designed by Alice Comyns Carr, was decorated with the iridescent wings of a thousand green jewel-beetles. Restored at the cost of £110,000, the dress was put on display in 2011 at Terry's home, Smallhythe Place.

Re-Creating Victor Hugo (p. 25)

Exiled from France in 1855, Hugo settled in Guernsey, where he bought Hauteville House the following year. He was responsible for the house's extraordinary interior design with its densely symbolic rooms moving upwards to a glazed, top-floor lookout. Many of Hugo's works were written here, including *Les Misérables*, which was turned into the famous musical 125 years later.

Postcards from Buxton, May 2019 (pp. 36-39)

Buxton owes much of its present form to successive Dukes of Devonshire, who built it up as a fashionable spa town in Georgian times and beyond. The *Crescent* was built as a hotel in the 1780s and in 2019 was undergoing substantial redevelopment. Its nearby stable block, also dating from the 1780s, was converted to a hospital in the 1880s when the spectacular dome was added, which was at the time the world's largest unsupported dome. Now known as the *Devonshire Dome*, it forms part of the University of Derby's Buxton campus, and boasts an astonishing echo which can be activated from its central point.

The tiny *Church of St Anne*, with its unexpected, exquisite Arts and Crafts interior, also hosts the grave of the 18th-century actor and comedian John Kane in its churchyard. After an agonising death, apparently, having eaten hemlock rather than horseradish, he was buried to face all the other graves: playing to his audience, as it were, in death as in life.

The *Pavilion Gardens*, lined on one side by an elegant run of Victorian buildings, were created by Sir Joseph Paxton and Edward Milner. The *Octagon*, designed by Robert Rippon Duke, hosted the Beatles in October 1963. The *Opera House*, built in 1903, was designed by the great theatre architect Frank Matcham, who was also responsible for London's Palladium and Coliseum.

Above the ancient limestone caves of *Poole's Cavern* rises Buxton Country Park, much of its landscape reclaimed from the spoil heaps of waste ash from 17th- and 18th-century lime-burning kilns. At the high point of Grin Low Hill stands *Solomon's Temple*, a Victorian folly commanding extensive, 360^0 views over Buxton and beyond.

Isles of Scilly: *Valhalla figureheads, Tresco Abbey Gardens* (p. 42)

The Valhalla collection contains over thirty ships' figureheads, nameboards and decorative carvings salvaged from shipwrecks around the coast of the Scillies. Most date from the mid to late nineteenth century.

The Disappeared (p. 69)

Until its restoration in the early 2010s, van Anthonissen's painting was known only as a representation of knots of people on a rather bleak beach. The revelation of its long-suppressed beached whale demanded a substantial interpretative shift and raised questions about why and when it had been painted out.

Trompe l'oeil (p. 71)

Rex Whistler's astonishing mural at Plas Newydd faces the dining-room windows, which command a stunning view across the Menai Straits and the mountains of Snowdonia. Whistler was killed in action in Normandy in July 1944.

Visions of War (p. 74)

The Sandham Memorial Chapel with its Stanley Spencer murals was commissioned in memory of Lt Henry Sandham, who died at the end of World War One, by his sister and her husband. Spencer based the murals on his own war experiences with the Royal Army Medical Corps in Bristol and Macedonia.